KEZA PAINTS A BRIGHT FUTURE

HOW WORKING TOGETHER CHANGES A VILLAGE

Story edited by Isaac Barnes

Photography courtesy of
Kenneth Burkey (40, 41, 42, 43), Elena Cret (45), Robby Doland (45),
Lydia Koehn (45), Chris McCurdy (45), Michael Rothermel (45)

KEZA PAINTS A BRIGHT FUTURE

HOW WORKING TOGETHER CHANGES A VILLAGE

Story by
Kenneth Burkey
Jill Heisey

Illustration by
Dale Vande Griend

My name is Keza. Mama says I've always been
an early riser. Each morning, I tiptoe past my sleeping
brother and slip outside in time to watch the sun
rise over Rwanda's rolling hills.

My village comes alive as the sunlight pokes and prods each sleepy corner. Hello, red motorcycles! Wake up, green grass! Rise and shine, yellow bananas! I close my eyes and can almost hear them reply, "Nice to see you again, Keza!"

It's the same scene every morning, but I still delight in the colors of the rising sun and everything it touches. I can't imagine anything more beautiful!

Soon after the sun peeks over the hills, a group of boys and girls about my age parades past in crisp, blue uniforms. In Rwanda, every student must wear a uniform, and blue is my favorite color of all—the color of Lake Kivu on a sunny day.

The children laugh and joke as they begin their daily walk to school. How lucky they are, learning to read and write! I'd like to join them, but a uniform costs five dollars, more than my family has right now. The children wave and greet me—"*Amakuru*, Keza!"—as they hurry on their way.

I wish I were on my way to school, but instead I return inside, where little Ganza is beginning to stir. The sun casts its rays through our windows and door, but I don't see any beautiful colors here.

Daylight reveals the brown mud walls that shelter us, the faded straw mats where we sleep, and our dirt floor, blackened by soot, where Mama tends the fire that cooks our porridge. Our home is happy but not beautiful.

When Papa calls me outside, the sight of green crops in the field makes me smile. He's teaching me to farm, just as his papa taught him. We grow cassava, beans, and potatoes. Most of the year, our family has enough to eat, but I know Papa and Mama worry about rain for the crops. Too little or too much means we will go hungry.

Papa and Mama work hard in the fields, but after feeding our family, there's little harvest left to sell in the market. Our family needs a good job. Mama sells bananas outside our house to earn a little extra money. Sometimes Papa finds work helping a neighbor harvest crops or replace a tattered roof, but those jobs last only a few days. Papa and Mama look discouraged, though they try not to show it.

I know that sending me to school is my parents' dream, as well as mine. If I go to school, Papa says, I can grow up to be anything. Rwanda needs scientists, teachers, doctors, and business people. And I could be one!

Papa saves as much as he can for my uniform.
But it seems there's always a doctor to pay or some
part of the house in desperate need of repair,
so my uniform must wait.

Once, during the rainy season, water poured
down from the sky like a river, soaking through
our roof and walls. Papa's savings got wet,
and the tattered bills were worthless.
He'd worked so hard for that money.
I almost went to school that year.

Papa tells me this year will
be different, and he seems excited.
Could that mean he's found a new job?

"Our church has been learning about savings groups," Papa explains. "Soon, we'll have enough money to make our own jobs. Come to the first meeting with me, Keza!" The church isn't far, just down a dusty path and over two hills.

The meeting begins with a greeting and a worship song I recognize from church. Our neighbor, Mama Claudine, prays, "God, please bless the work of our hands. Thank You for the skills You have given us, and help us to remember that You have given us each other." The savings group leader shares a lesson from the Bible.

After the Bible lesson, one by one, each person puts 50 cents into a lockbox for safekeeping and records their contribution in their passbook. When the last person has given, the group has over 12 dollars!

Instead of taking turns borrowing the money, Papa's group votes to start one business, all together.

The group leader invites ideas. "What about a painting business?" Papa suggests, smiling at me. He knows how much I love color! There are many good ideas, but when the group votes, they agree to begin "Painting the Future." On the walk home, I'm lost in a daydream, picturing my whole village painted with bright colors!

With everyone working together, it takes two months to save enough to buy the brushes and rollers, as well as the dye and cassava flour to make the paint.

Now, Painting the Future is open for business and starting its first job: painting our church. Papa lets me help as the group mixes sky blue paint and rolls it on the church walls in careful strokes. Everyone takes a turn!

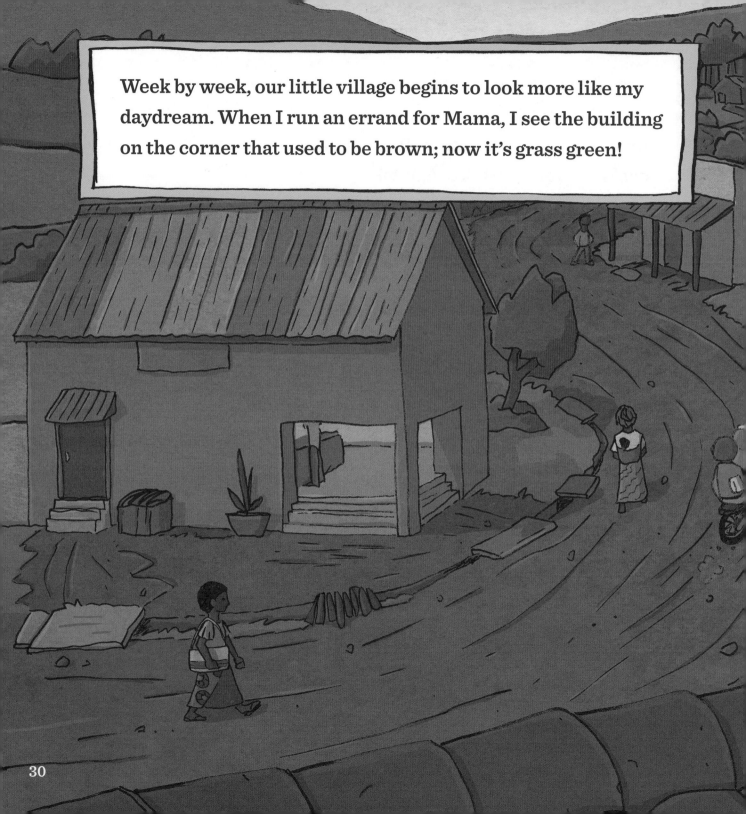

Week by week, our little village begins to look more like my daydream. When I run an errand for Mama, I see the building on the corner that used to be brown; now it's grass green!

It's easy to spot the banana-yellow pharmacy, and I smile as I pass the motorcycle-red restaurant down the road. This is the work of my papa's hands, and I can't imagine anything more beautiful!

CHEZ MAMA KALIZA

I pass three more colorful buildings as I head for home. "Keza!" Papa calls to me as I come into view. He's home early, and for a moment, I'm worried that he's run out of work. But he's smiling. "I've mixed a very special batch of paint," he says. "You're just in time to help me."

"Today we're going to paint our home." Together, we paint our house bright orange! With each brush stroke, my smile grows wider. The sun is beginning to sink low in the sky as we step back to admire our work.

In awe, I whisper to Papa, "I can't imagine anything more beautiful."

When I've finished cleaning the brushes, Papa and Mama call me into the house. There's a new blue mosquito net over our sleeping mats and a bright yellow water filter in the corner. A basket on the table overflows with yellow pineapples and red mangoes.

But there is one more surprise.
In their hands, Mama and Papa are holding a crisp,
blue uniform. A squeal of delight escapes my lips!

I fling my arms around my parents as I imagine myself walking to school with my friends, learning to read and writing my own name. "*Murakoze*, Mama and Papa! Thank you!"

It's almost bedtime, but I try on my uniform to
make sure I'll be ready for my first day of school.
It fits perfectly, like it was made just for me.
I turn to show my proud papa and mama.

"How does it look?" I ask. Mama's eyes flood with happy tears as she whispers a quiet prayer of thanks to God. Papa takes a moment to compose himself before he speaks. "We can't imagine anything more beautiful!"

Challenges in Rwanda

While Rwanda has made significant economic progress in the last two decades, over 60 percent of the population continues to live on less than $1.90 a day.[1]

Vulnerable Rwandan households—especially those in rural communities—still lack access to many opportunities, including basic financial services like a safe place to save their money. The government, local churches, and the people of Rwanda are working together to create unity and eradicate poverty.

QUICK FACTS[2]

⮕ *Over 11 million people live in Rwanda.*

⮕ *Rwanda is the most densely populated country in Africa.*

⮕ *About 75 percent of the population engages in subsistence agriculture.*

⮕ *Rwanda is known as the "Land of a Thousand Hills."*

1. United Nations Development Programme
2. CIA World Factbook

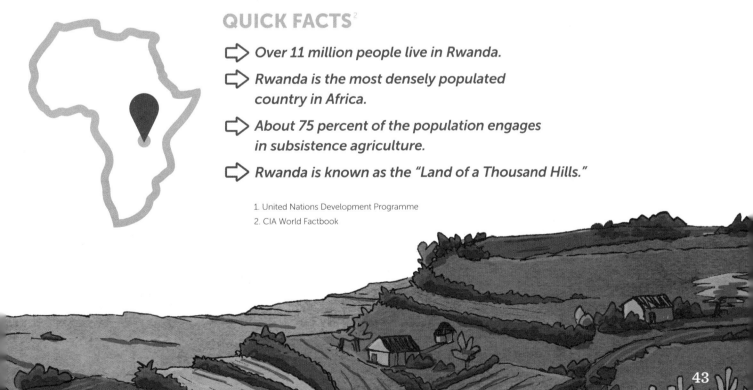

HOPE in Rwanda

HOPE Rwanda works in partnership with Rwandan church denominations to facilitate savings group programs. In these savings groups, volunteer church facilitators share the Gospel, lead Bible studies, and provide training to members, who regularly save money together. HOPE Rwanda members then use their savings or take out loans from their group to stabilize household income, provide a safety net in emergencies, start or expand businesses, or pay for routine expenses such as school supplies for their children.

To further invest in the dreams of Rwandan families, HOPE International also provides Christ-centered financial services through its microfinance institution Urwego Bank.

THE GOOD SHEPHERDS SAVINGS GROUP

The story of Keza and her father's savings group was inspired by an actual HOPE International savings group in Byumba, Rwanda. The Good Shepherds savings group began in 2016 and soon launched a shared painting business, using an old recipe that combined locally-sourced ingredients like cassava flour, ground chalk, water, oil, and dye. The savings group members, as well as the village, have been transformed as, together, they save their money, worship God, and work alongside one another. In community, they're growing deeper in relationship with one another and generating steady work and consistent income to meet the needs of their families.

All proceeds from *Keza Paints a Bright Future* will support the work of HOPE International in Rwanda and around the world.

HOPE International invests in the dreams of families in the world's underserved communities as we proclaim and live the Gospel.

We share the hope of Christ as we provide discipleship, biblically based training, a safe place to save, and loans that restore dignity for those living in poverty. We serve as a network of microfinance institutions and savings group programs, similar to the one portrayed in *Keza Paints a Bright Future.* HOPE works in Africa, Asia, Eastern Europe, and Latin America.

To learn more about HOPE International, visit **www.hopeinternational.org.**

Zambia

Ukraine

Dominican Republic

South Asia

Philippines

HOPE
INTERNATIONAL ®

Investing in dreams.

www.hopeinternational.org